DAVE G

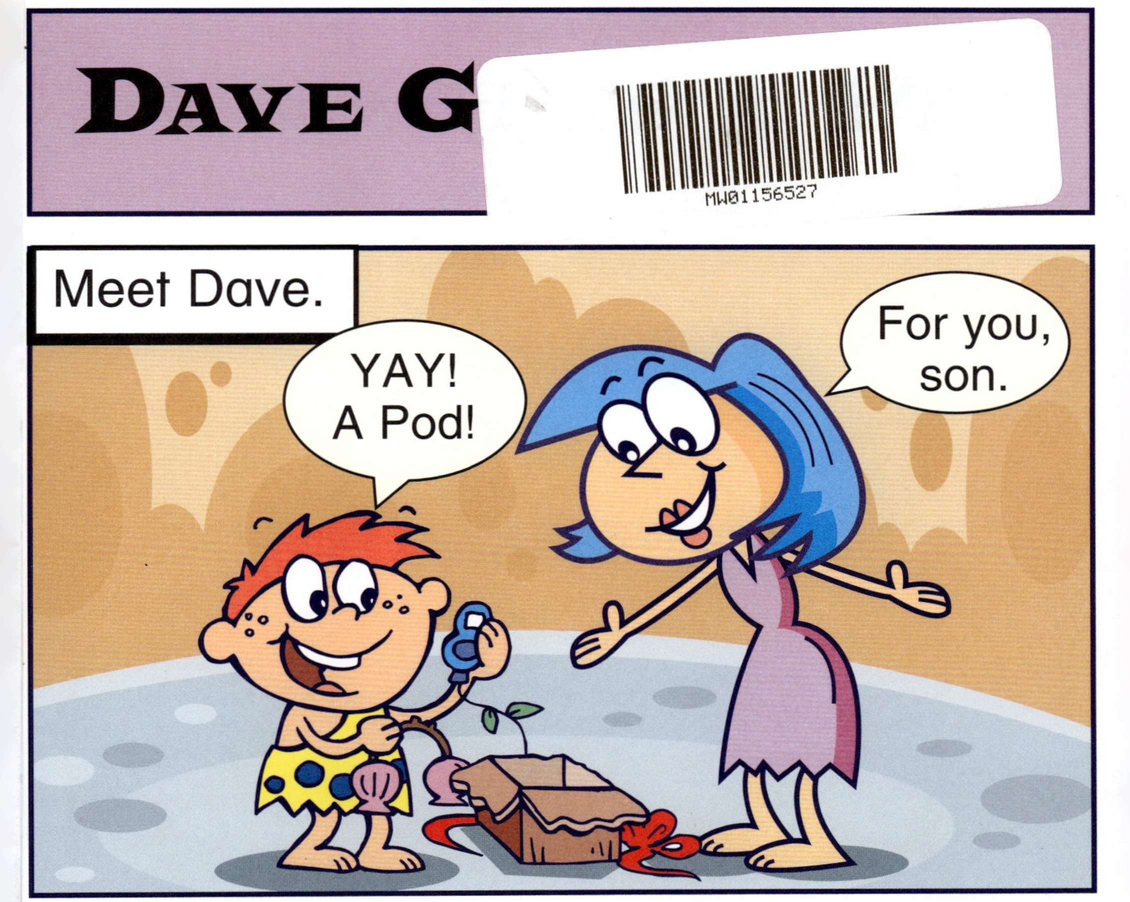
Meet Dave.
YAY! A Pod!
For you, son.

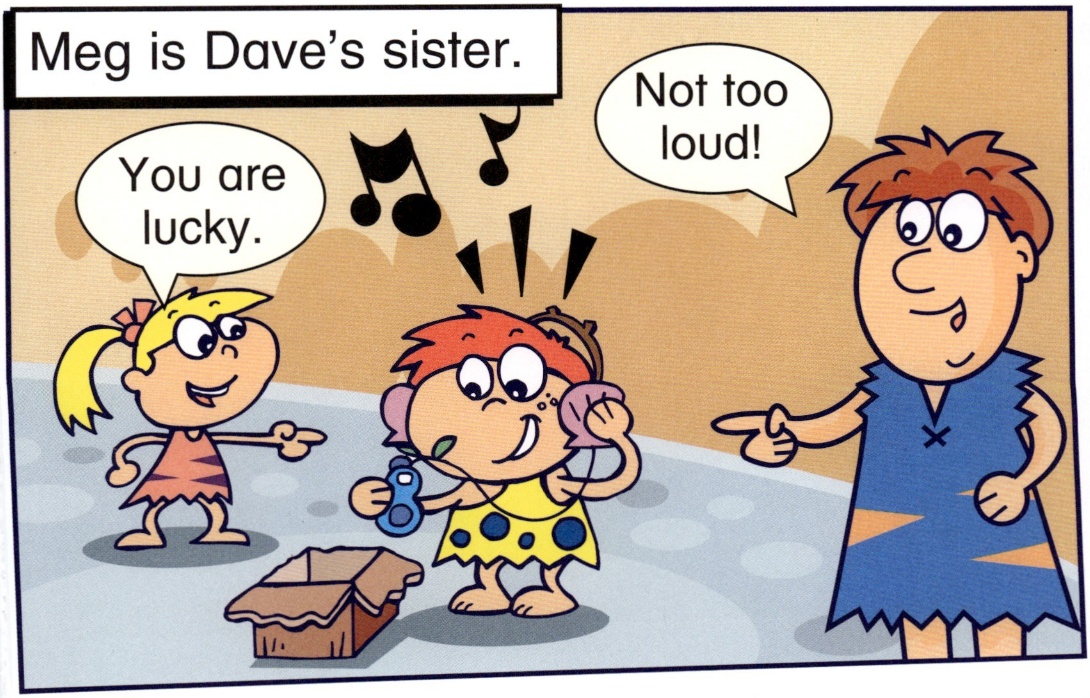
Meg is Dave's sister.
You are lucky.
Not too loud!

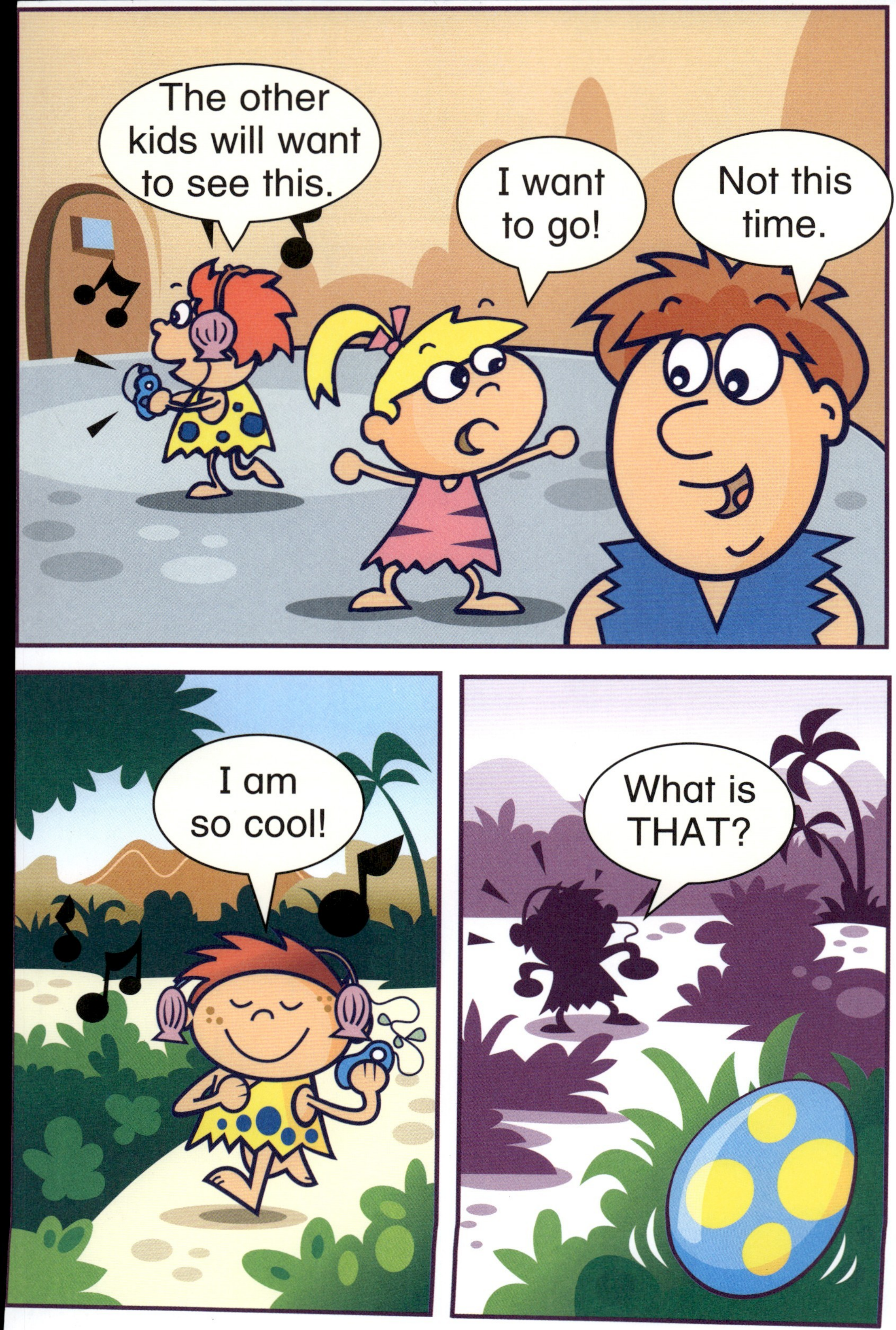
The other kids will want to see this.
I want to go!
Not this time.
I am so cool!
What is THAT?

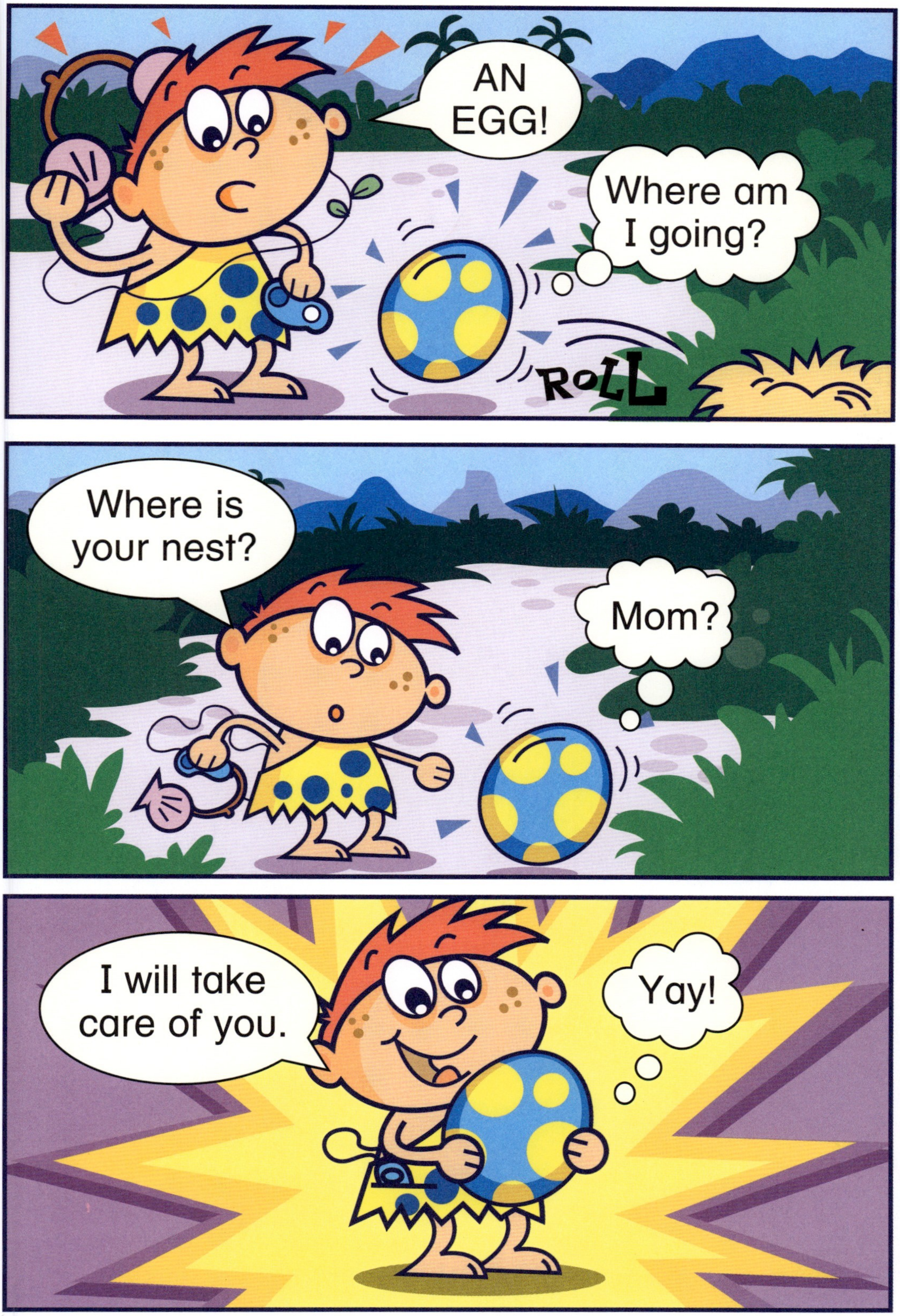
AN EGG!
Where am I going?
ROLL
Where is your nest?
Mom?
I will take care of you.
Yay!

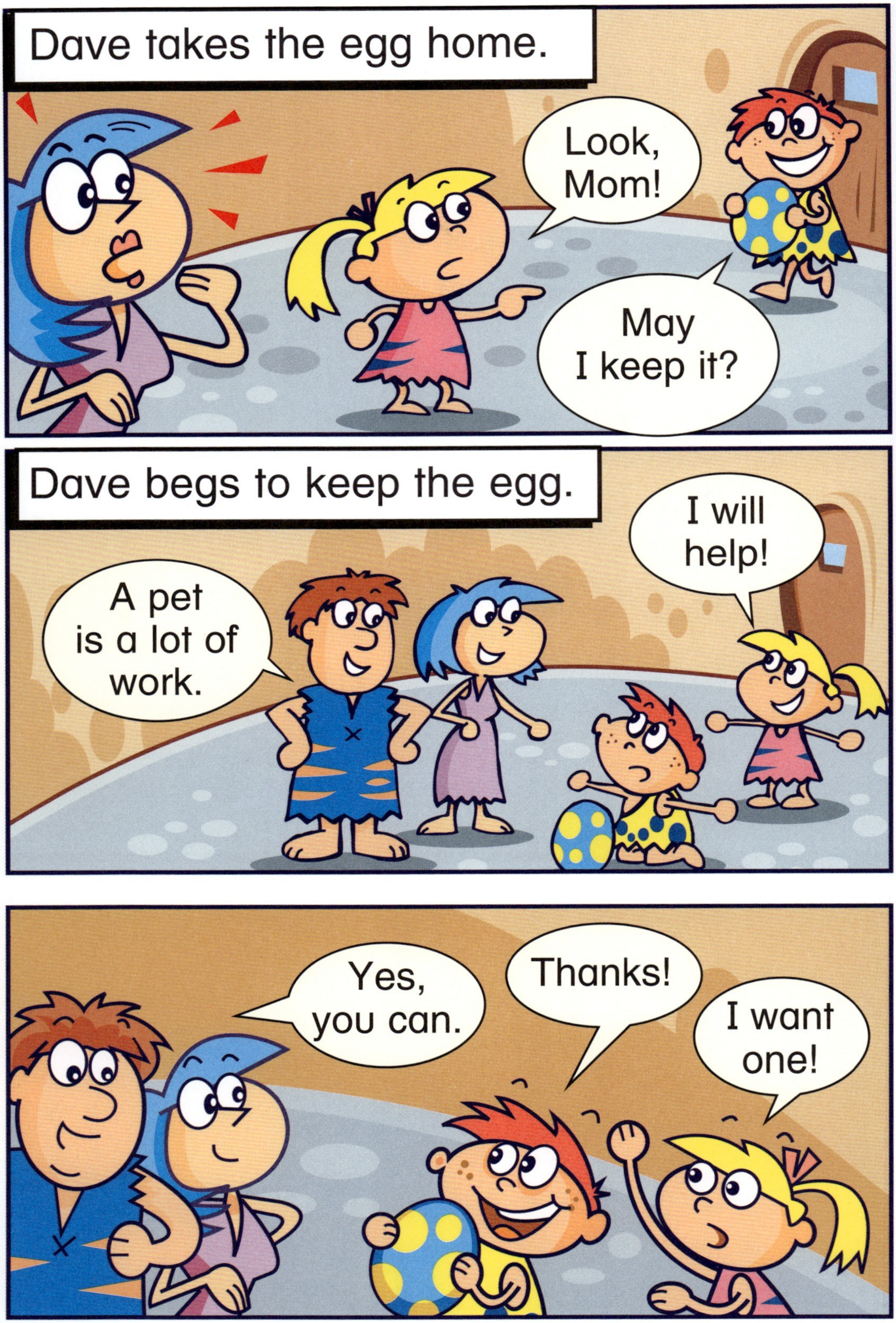
Dave takes the egg home.
Look, Mom!
May I keep it?
Dave begs to keep the egg.
I will help!
A pet is a lot of work.
Yes, you can.
Thanks!
I want one!

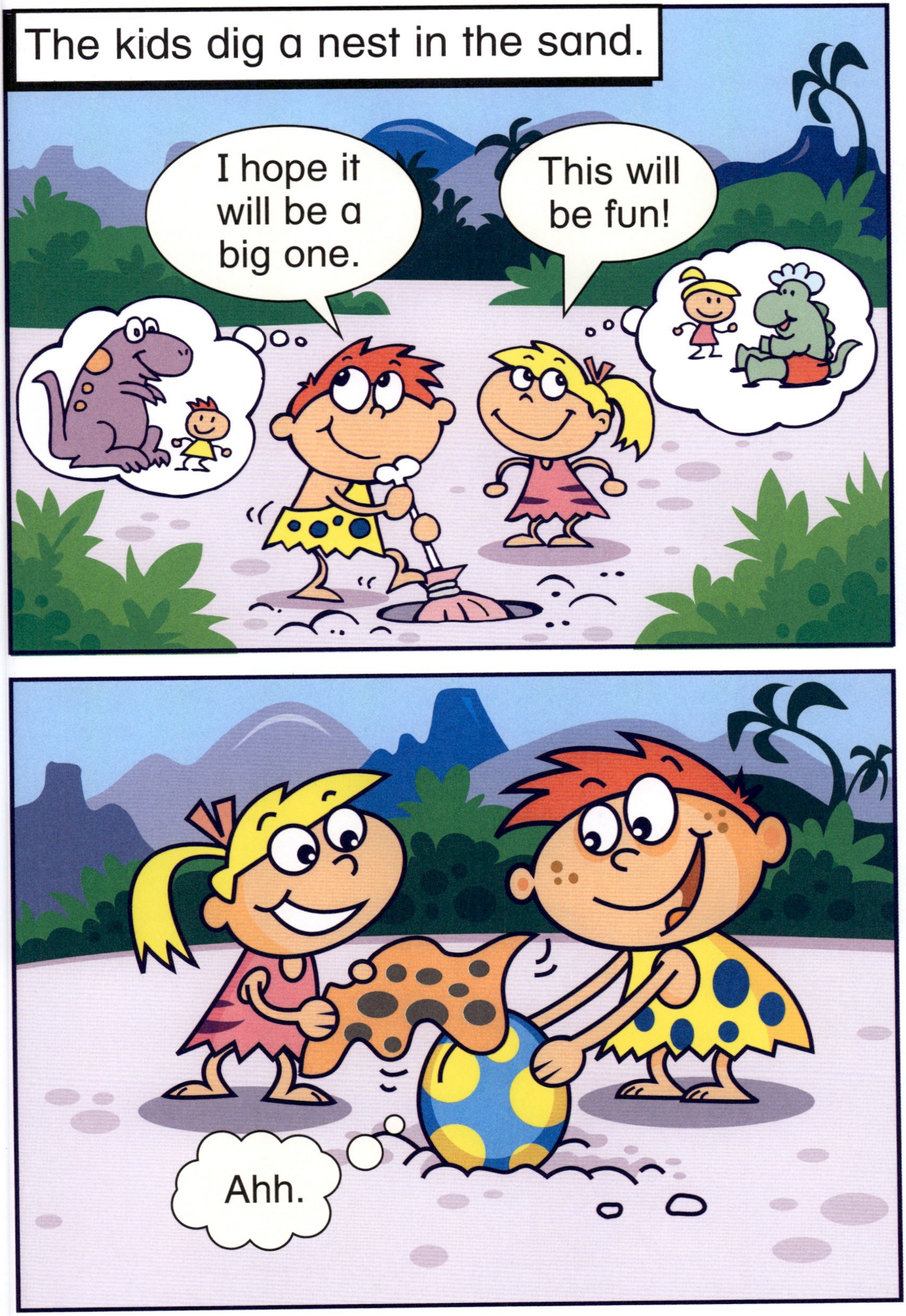
The kids dig a nest in the sand.
I hope it will be a big one.
This will be fun!
Ahh.

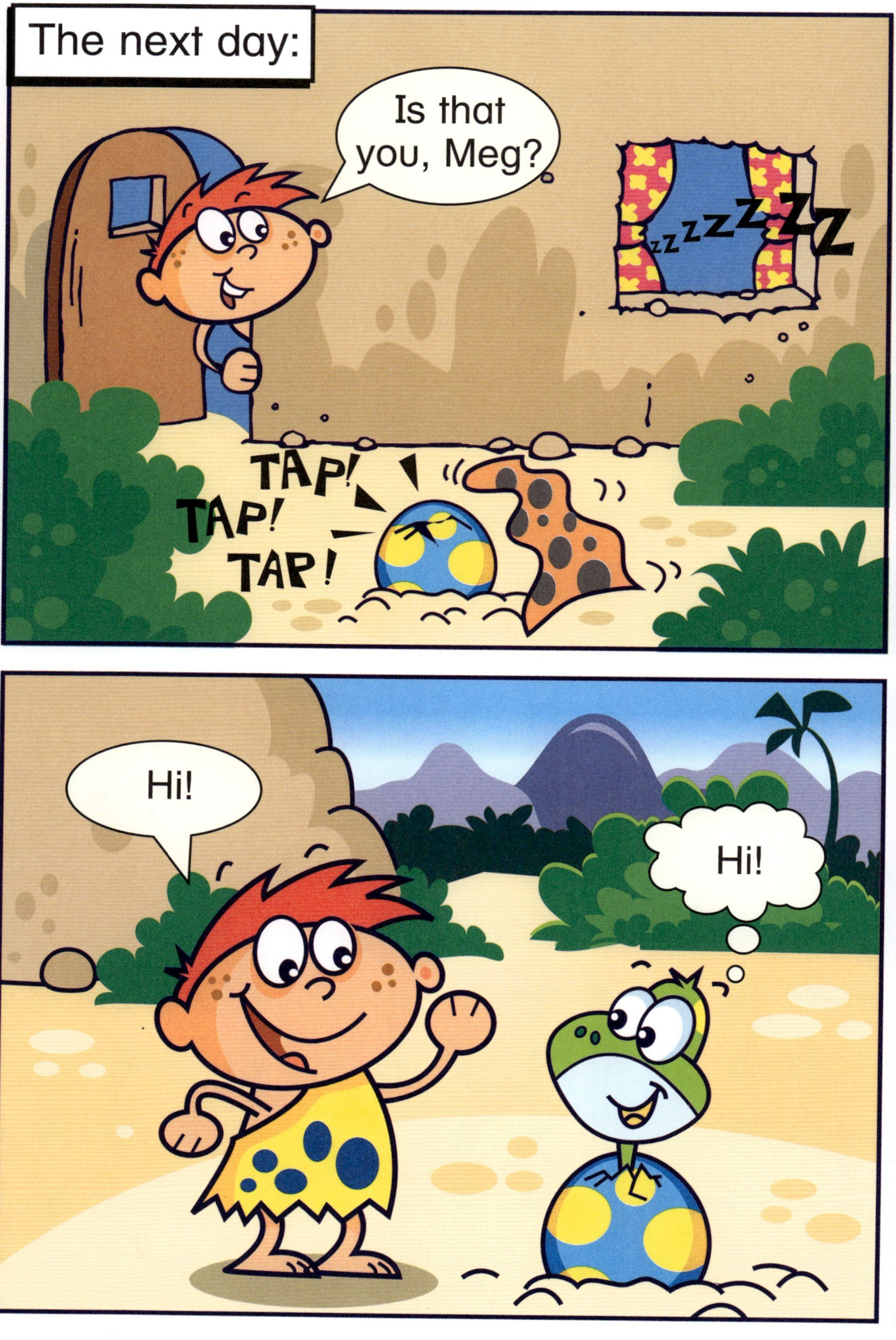
The next day:
Is that you, Meg?
TAP!
TAP!
TAP!
Hi!
Hi!

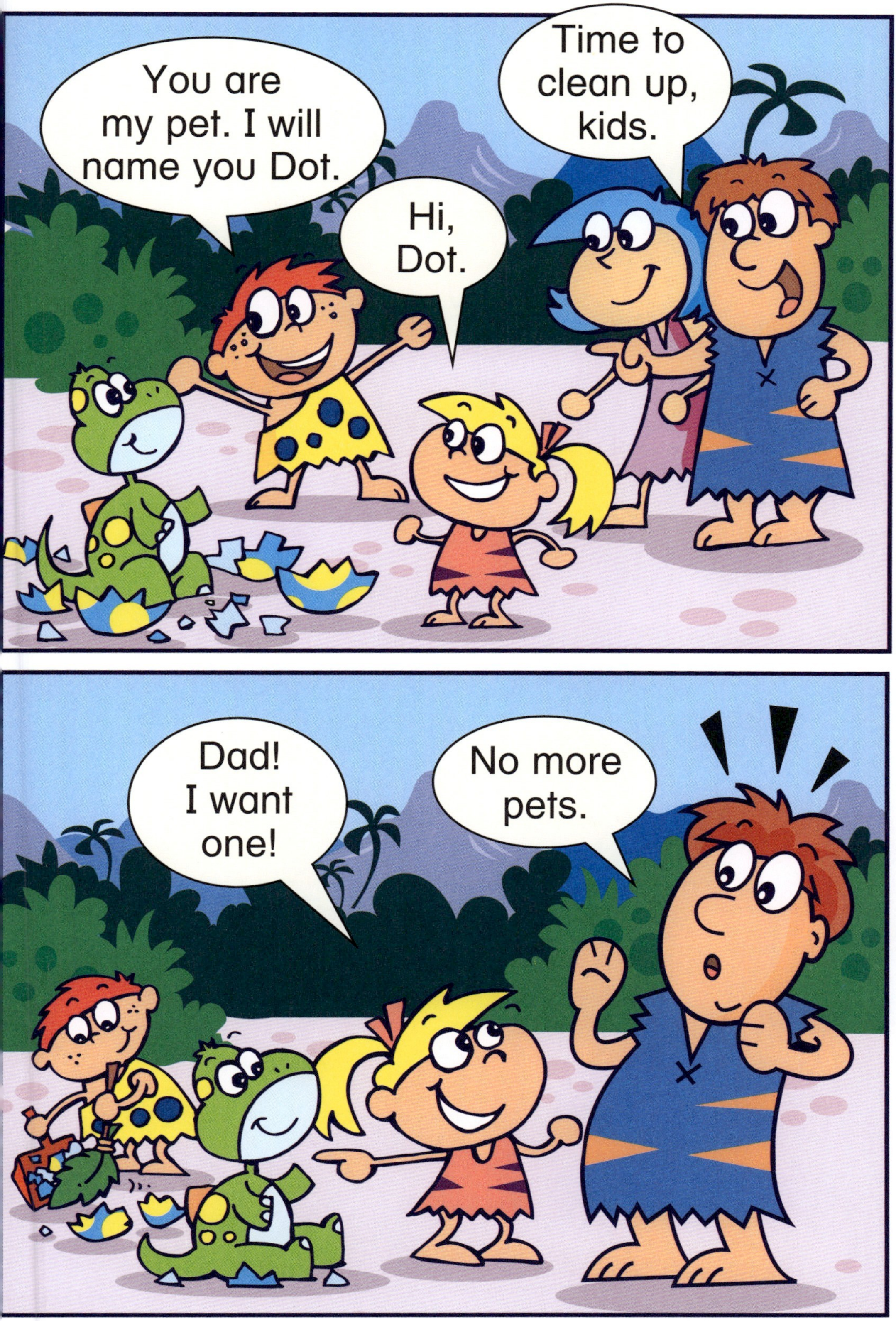
You are my pet. I will name you Dot.
Hi, Dot.
Time to clean up, kids.
Dad! I want one!
No more pets.

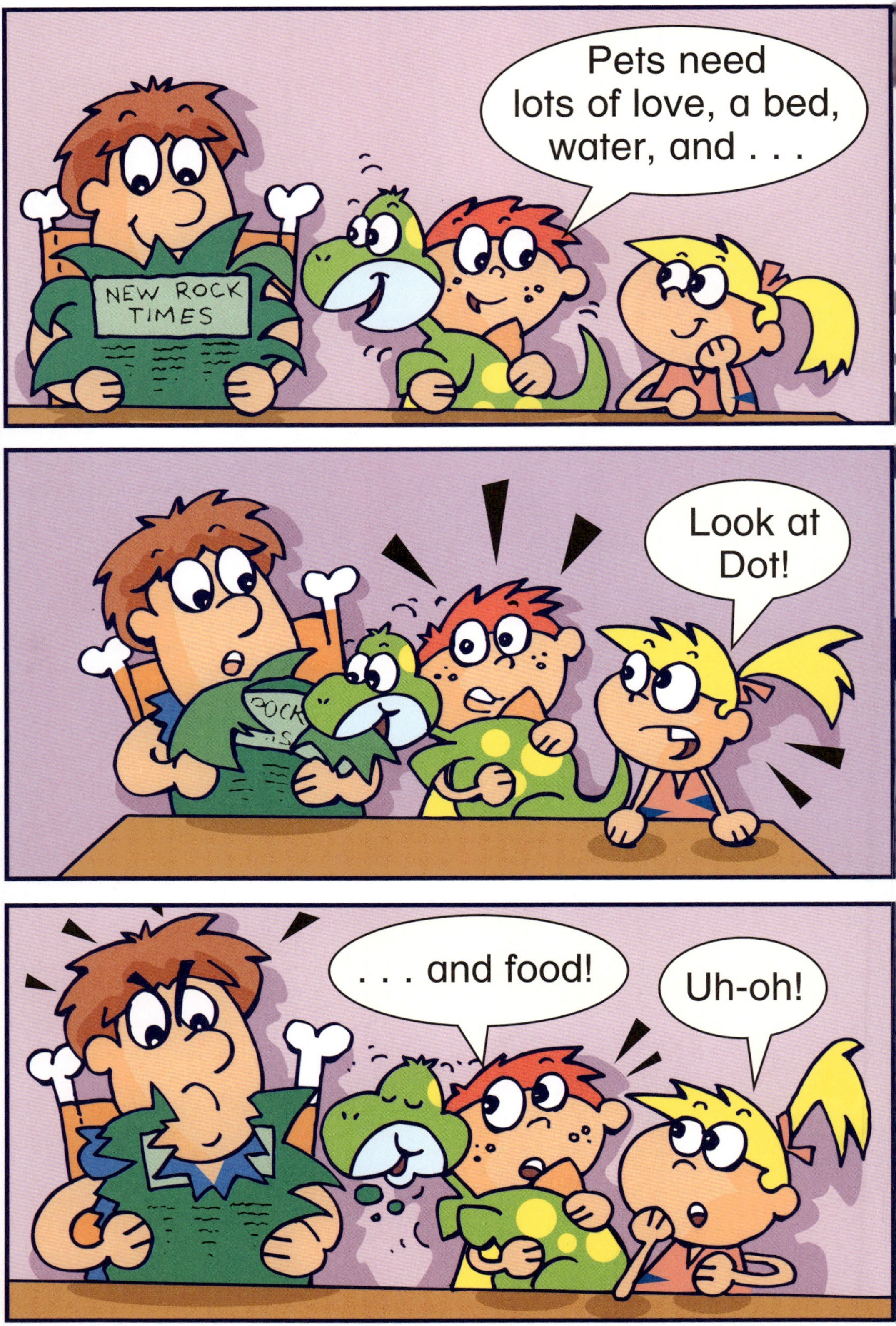
NEW ROCK TIMES
Pets need lots of love, a bed, water, and . . .
Look at Dot!
. . . and food!
Uh-oh!

The Big Dig

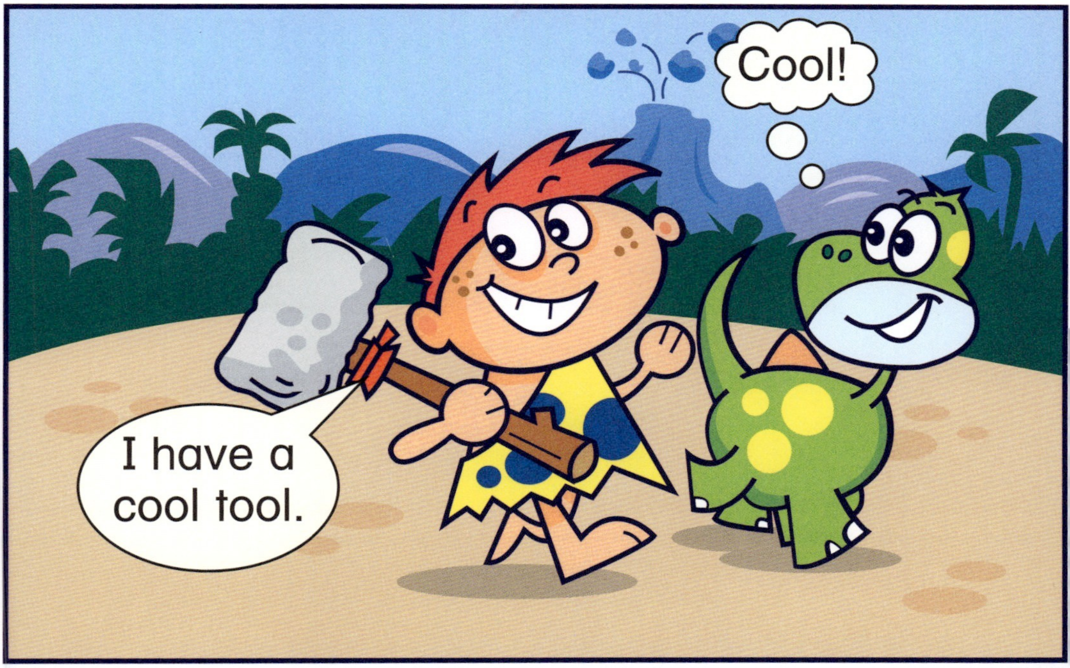
Cool!
I have a cool tool.

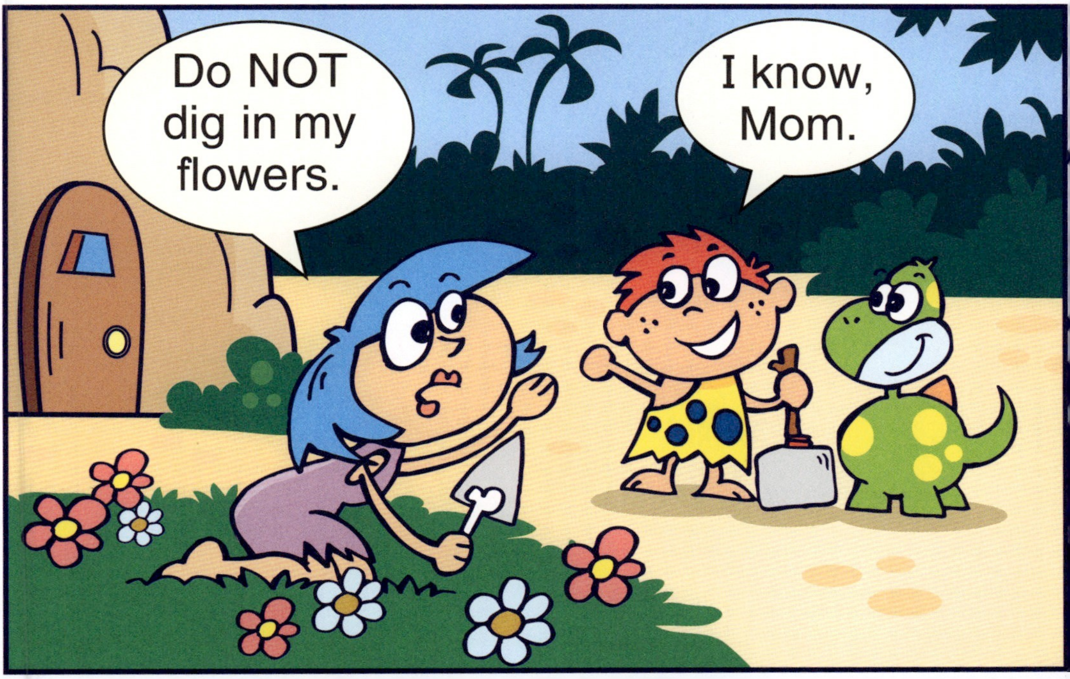
Do NOT dig in my flowers.
I know, Mom.

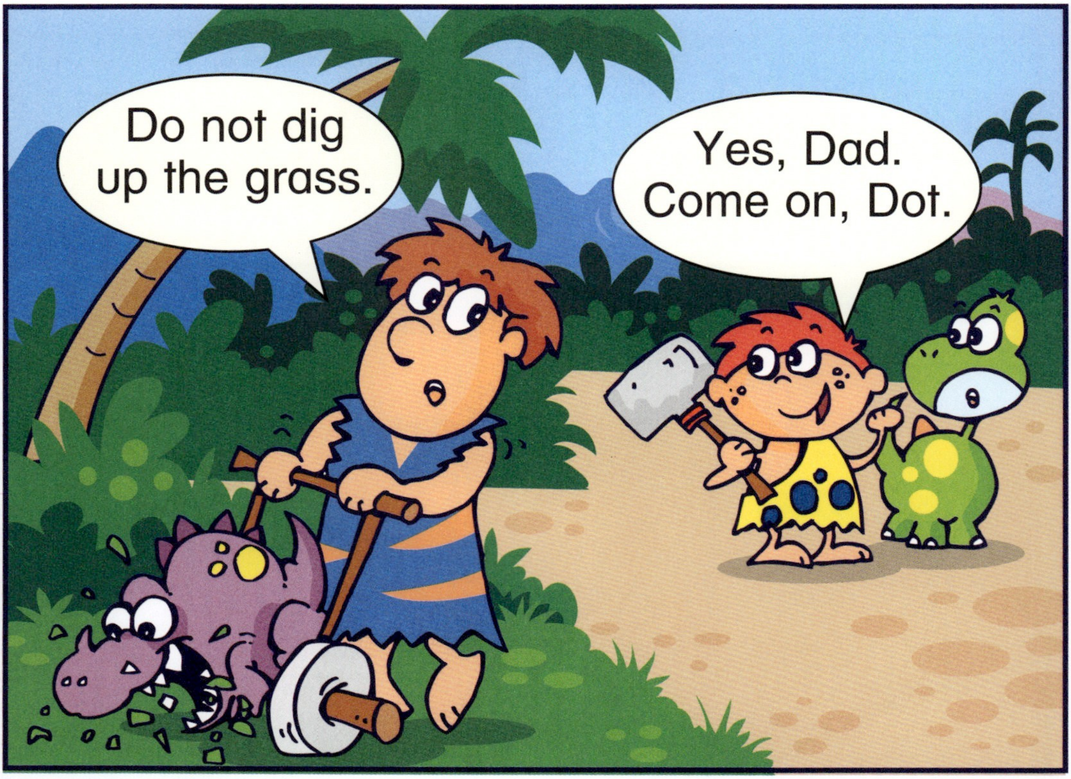
Do not dig up the grass.
Yes, Dad. Come on, Dot.

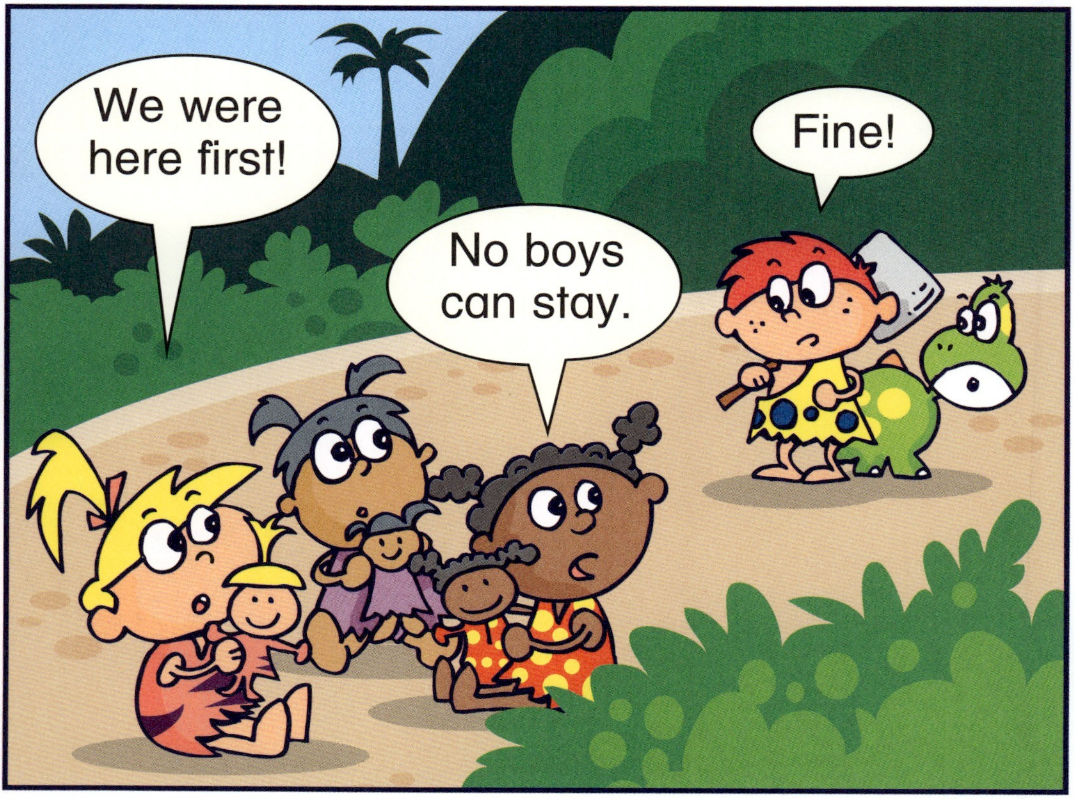
We were here first!
No boys can stay.
Fine!

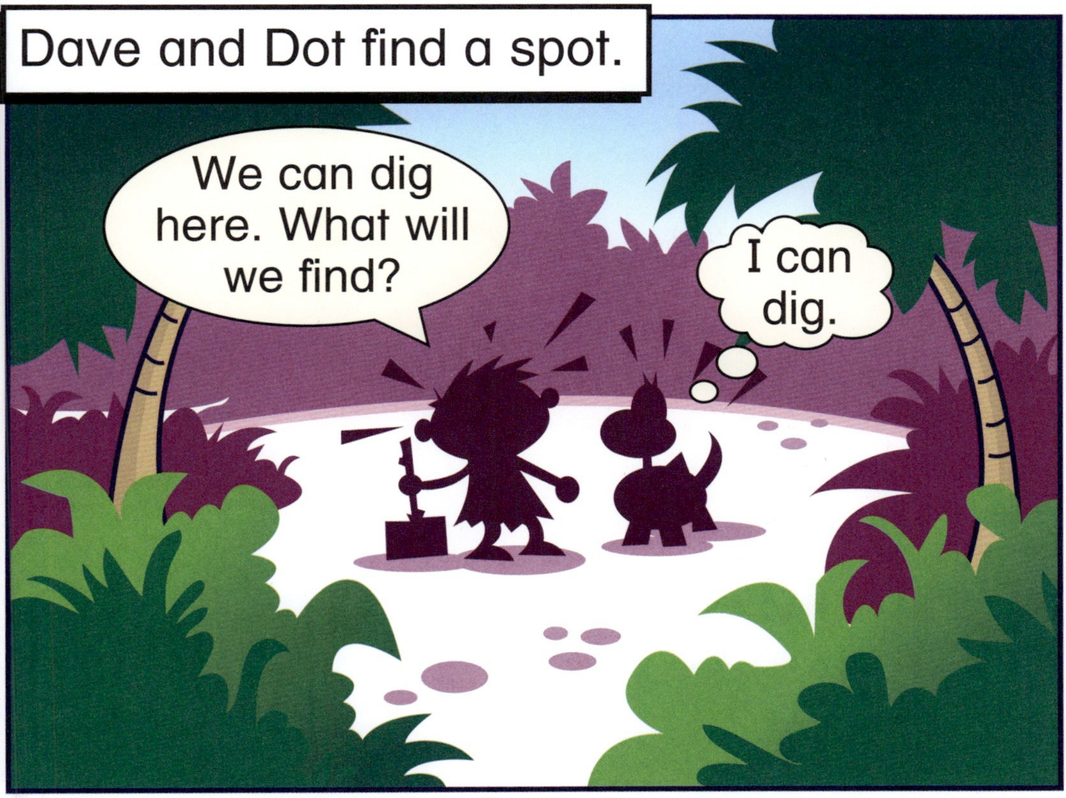
Dave and Dot find a spot.
We can dig here. What will we find?
I can dig.

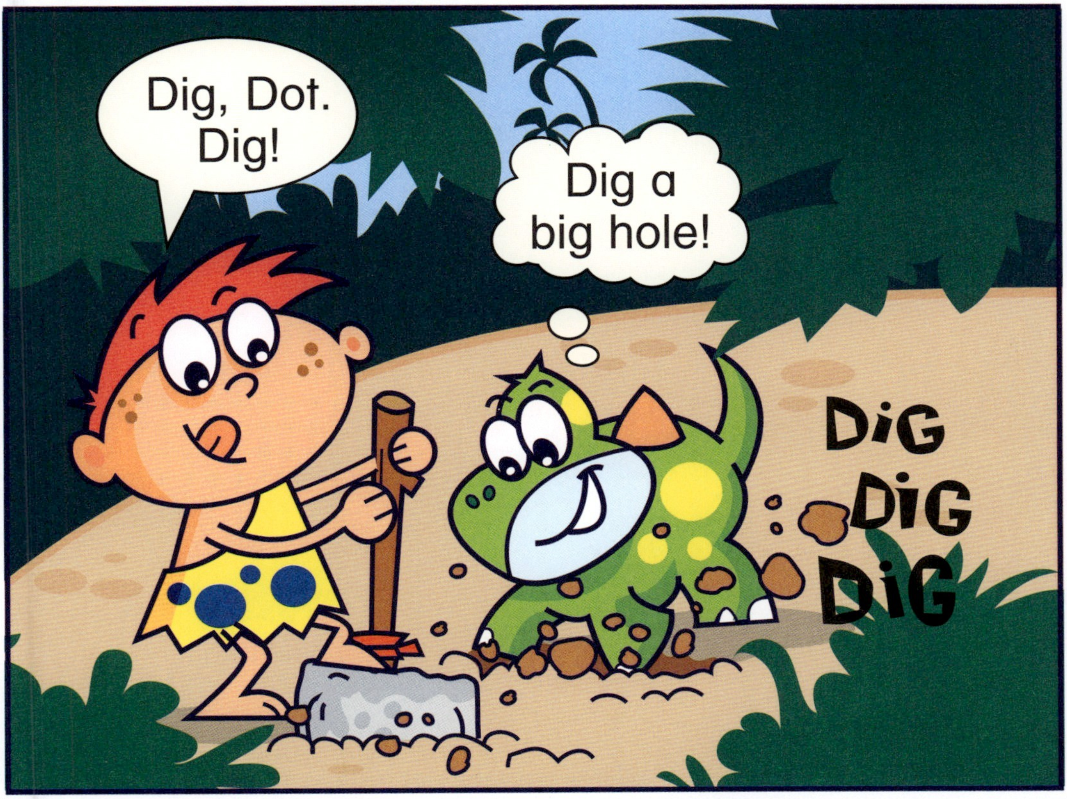
Dig, Dot. Dig!
Dig a big hole!
DiG DiG DiG

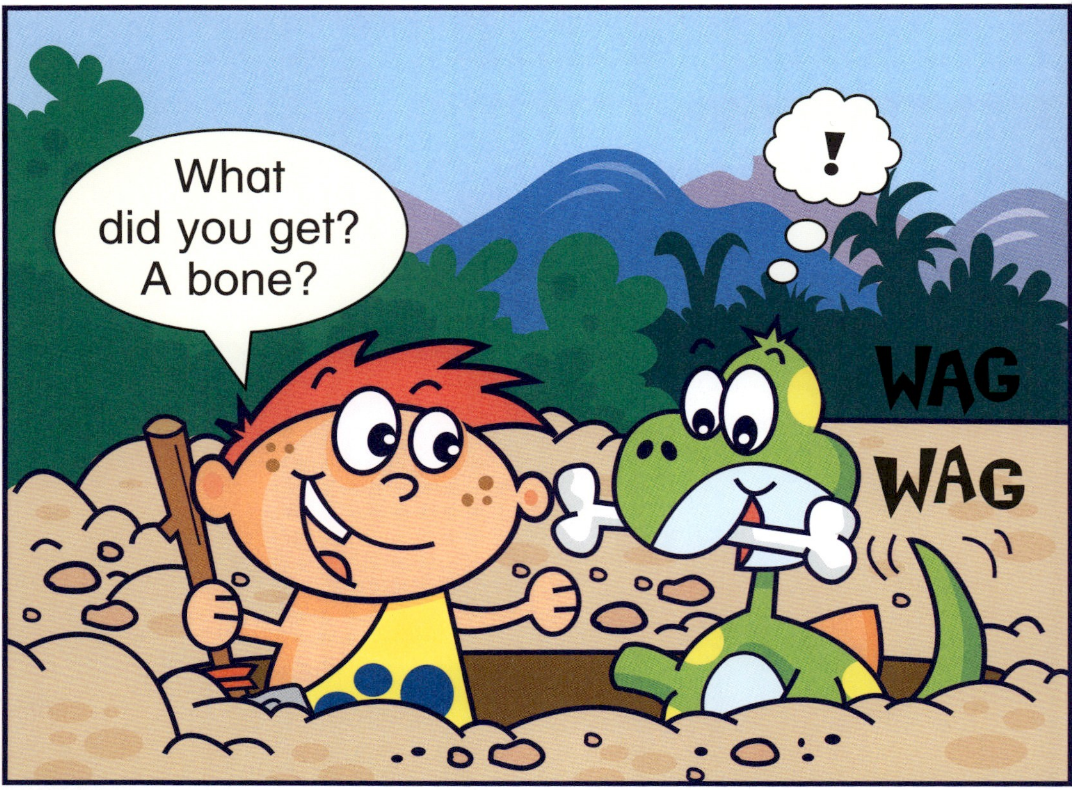
What did you get? A bone?
!
WAG
WAG

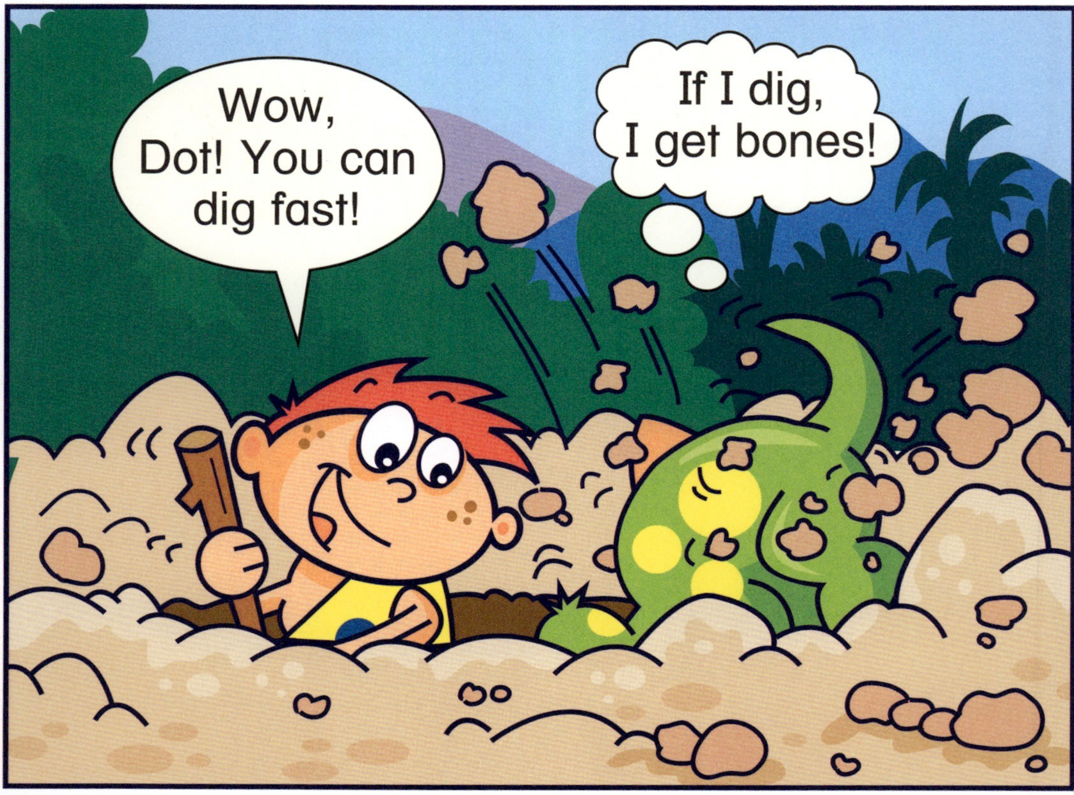
Wow, Dot! You can dig fast!
If I dig, I get bones!

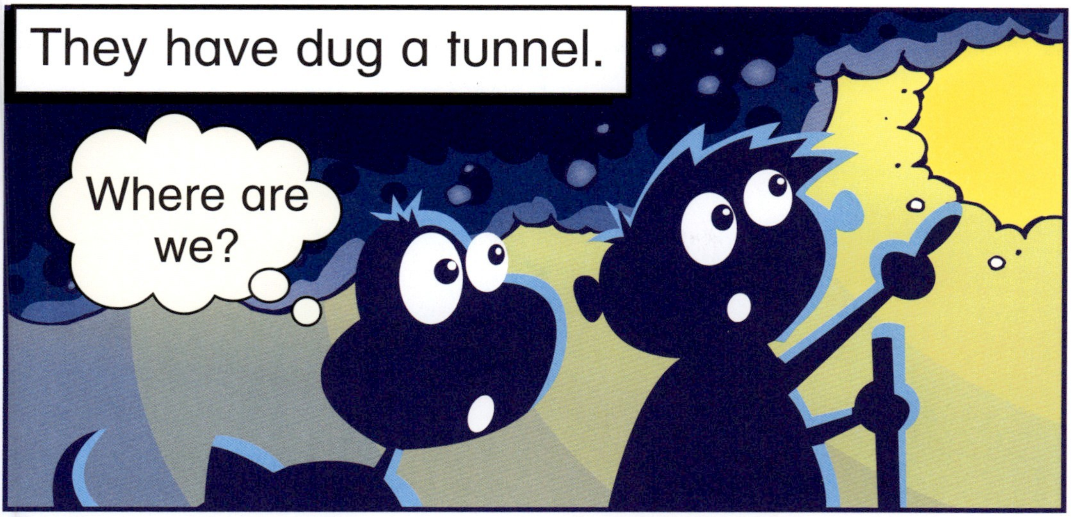
They have dug a tunnel.
Where are we?

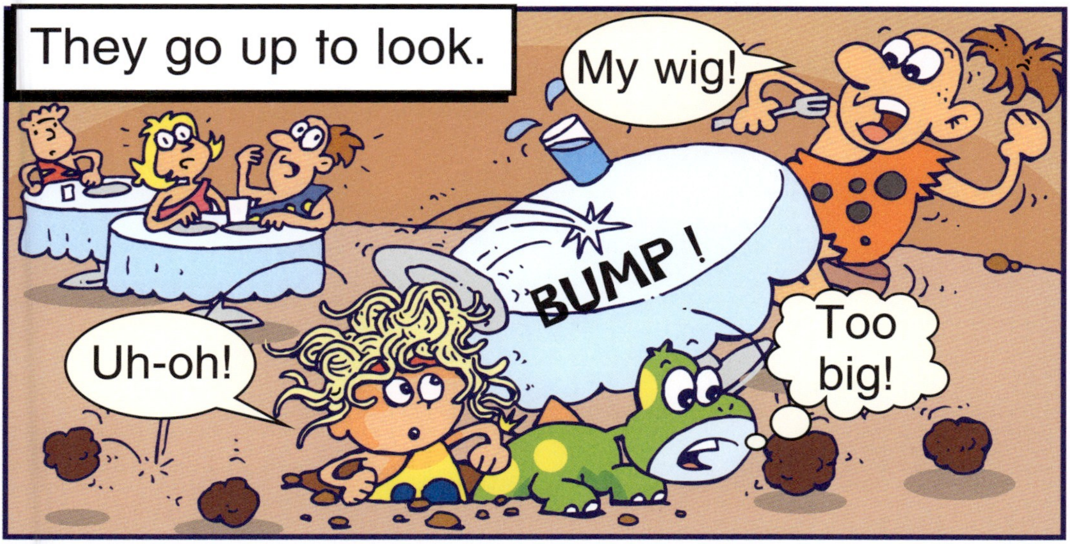
They go up to look.
My wig!
BUMP!
Uh-oh!
Too big!

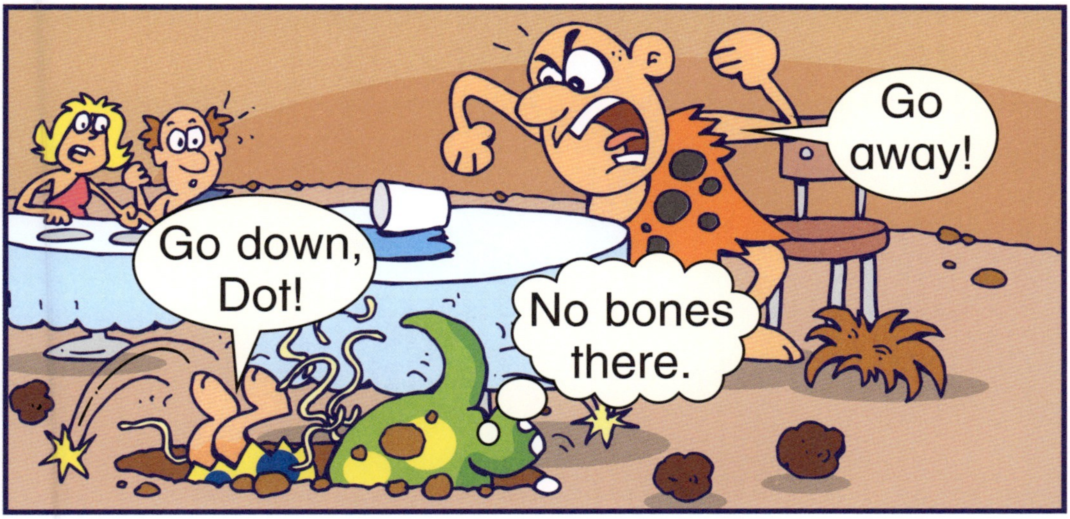
Go away!
Go down, Dot!
No bones there.

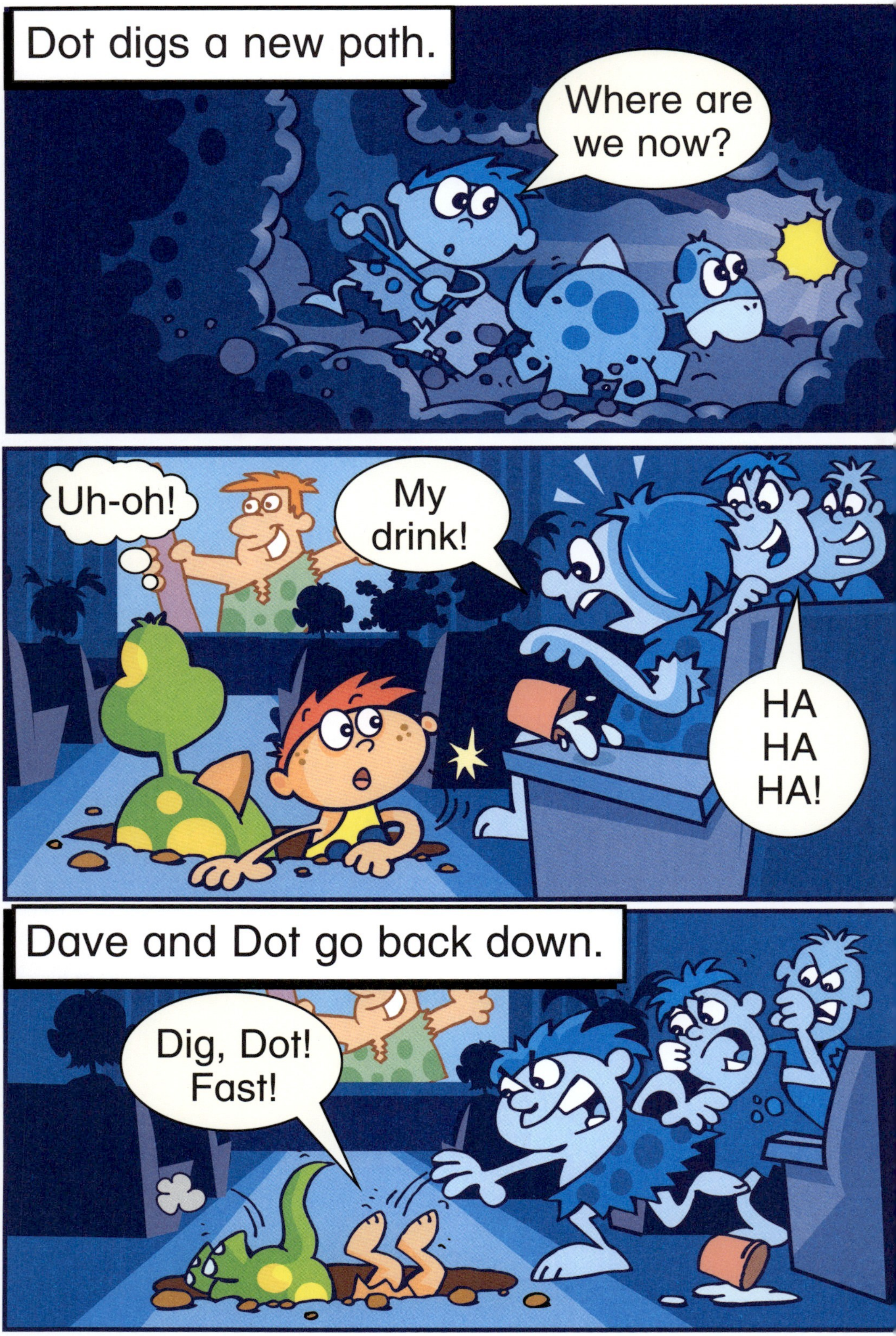
Dot digs a new path.
Where are we now?
Uh-oh!
My drink!
HA HA HA!
Dave and Dot go back down.
Dig, Dot! Fast!

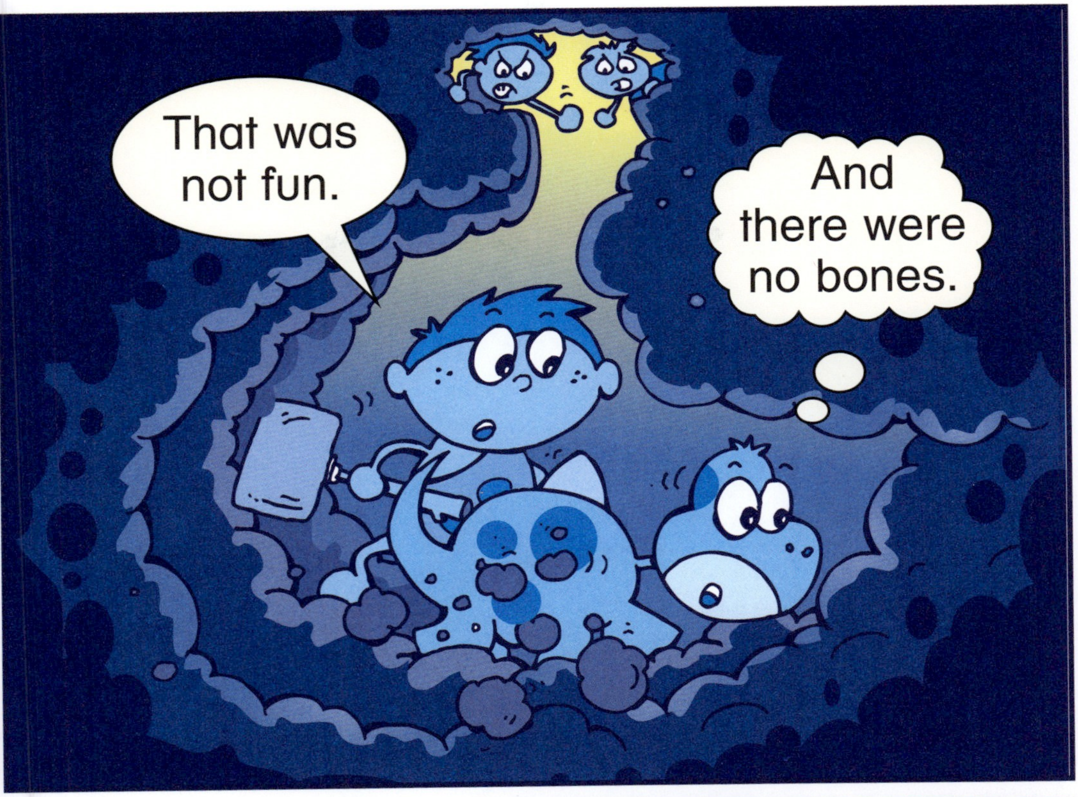
That was not fun.
And there were no bones.

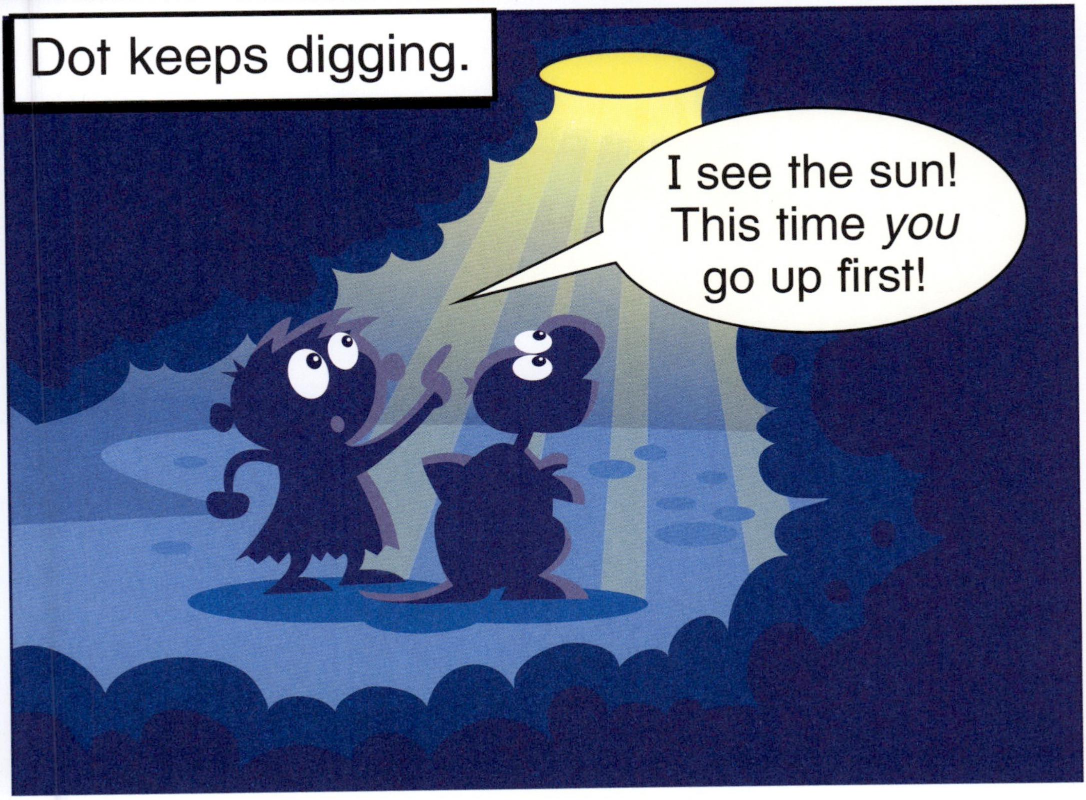
Dot keeps digging.
I see the sun! This time *you* go up first!

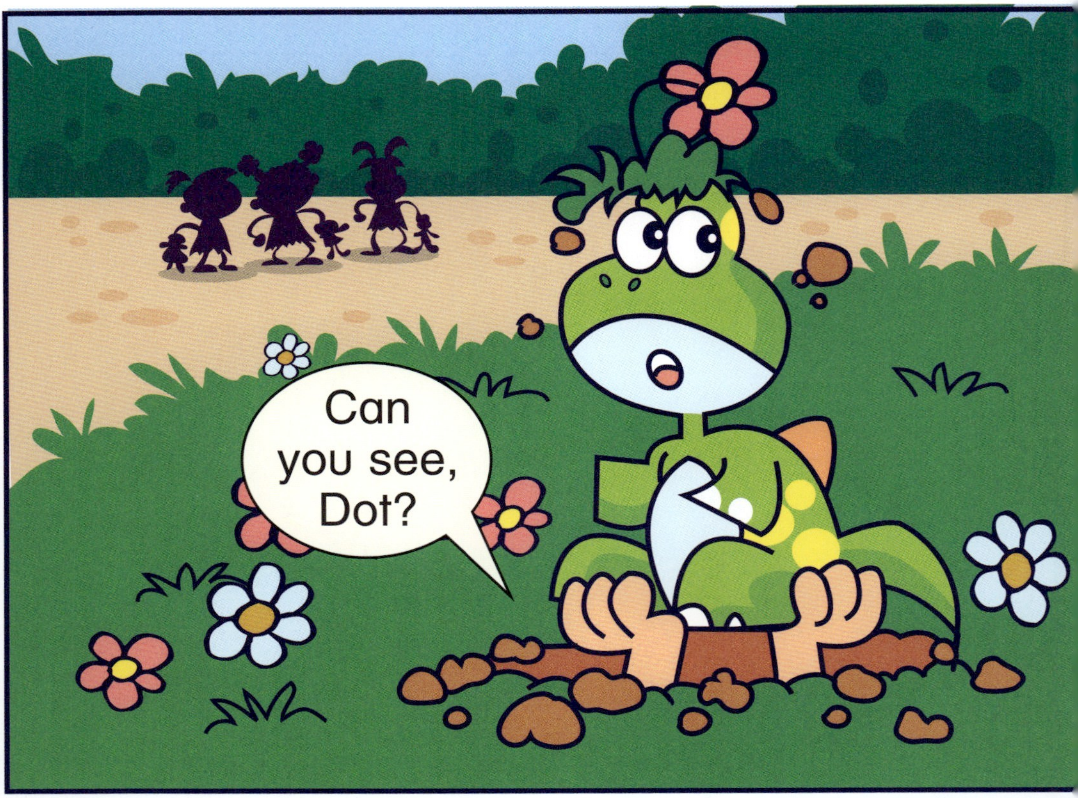
Can you see, Dot?

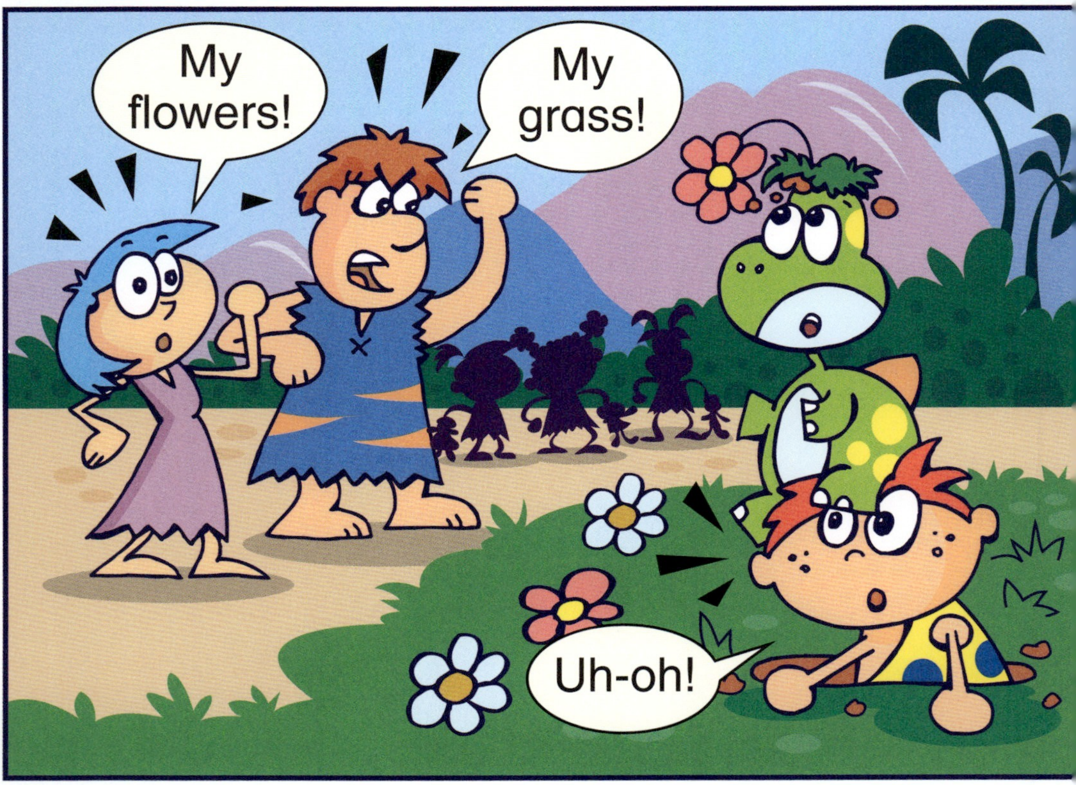
My flowers!
My grass!
Uh-oh!

THE FOG BOG

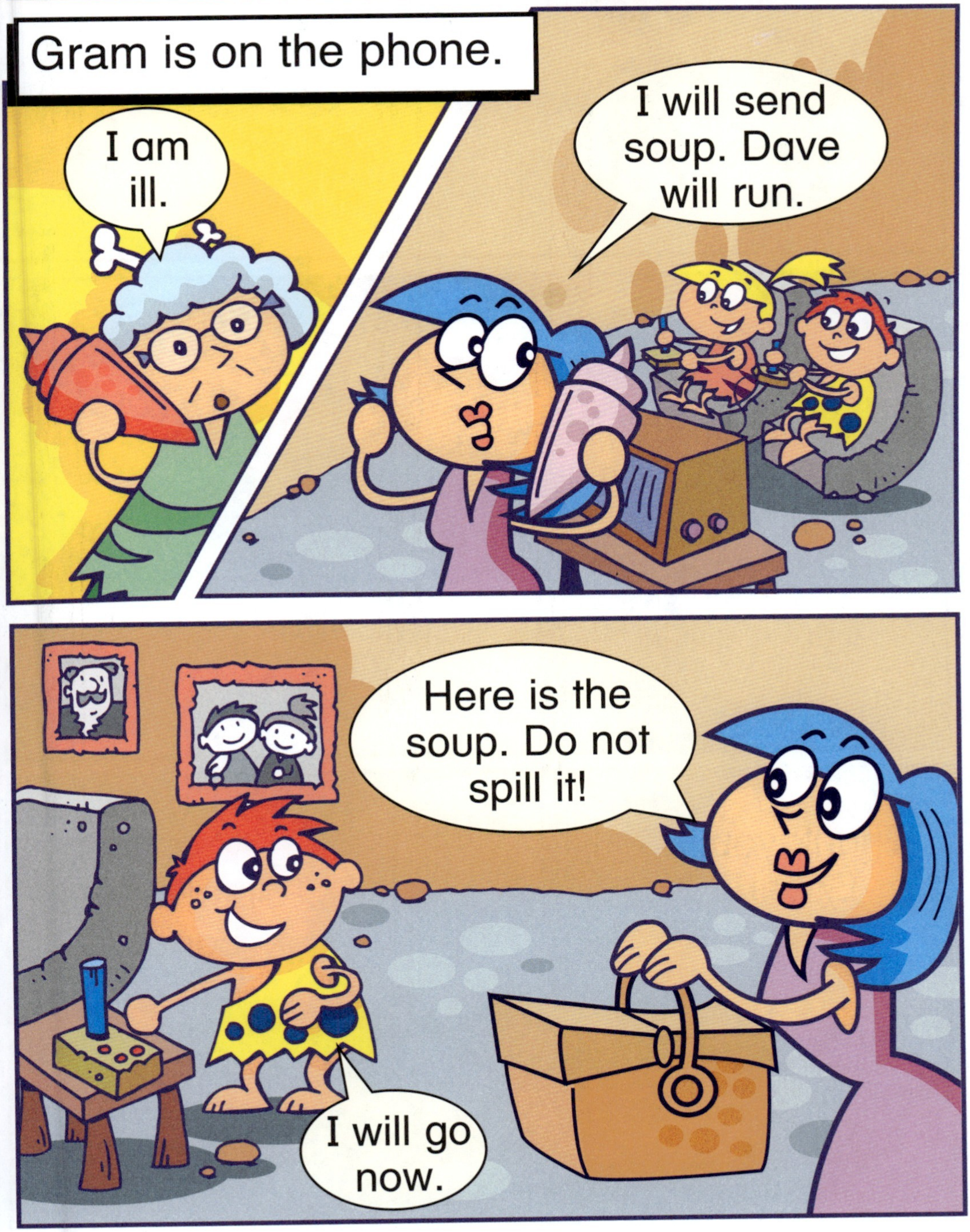
Gram is on the phone.
I am ill.
I will send soup. Dave will run.
Here is the soup. Do not spill it!
I will go now.

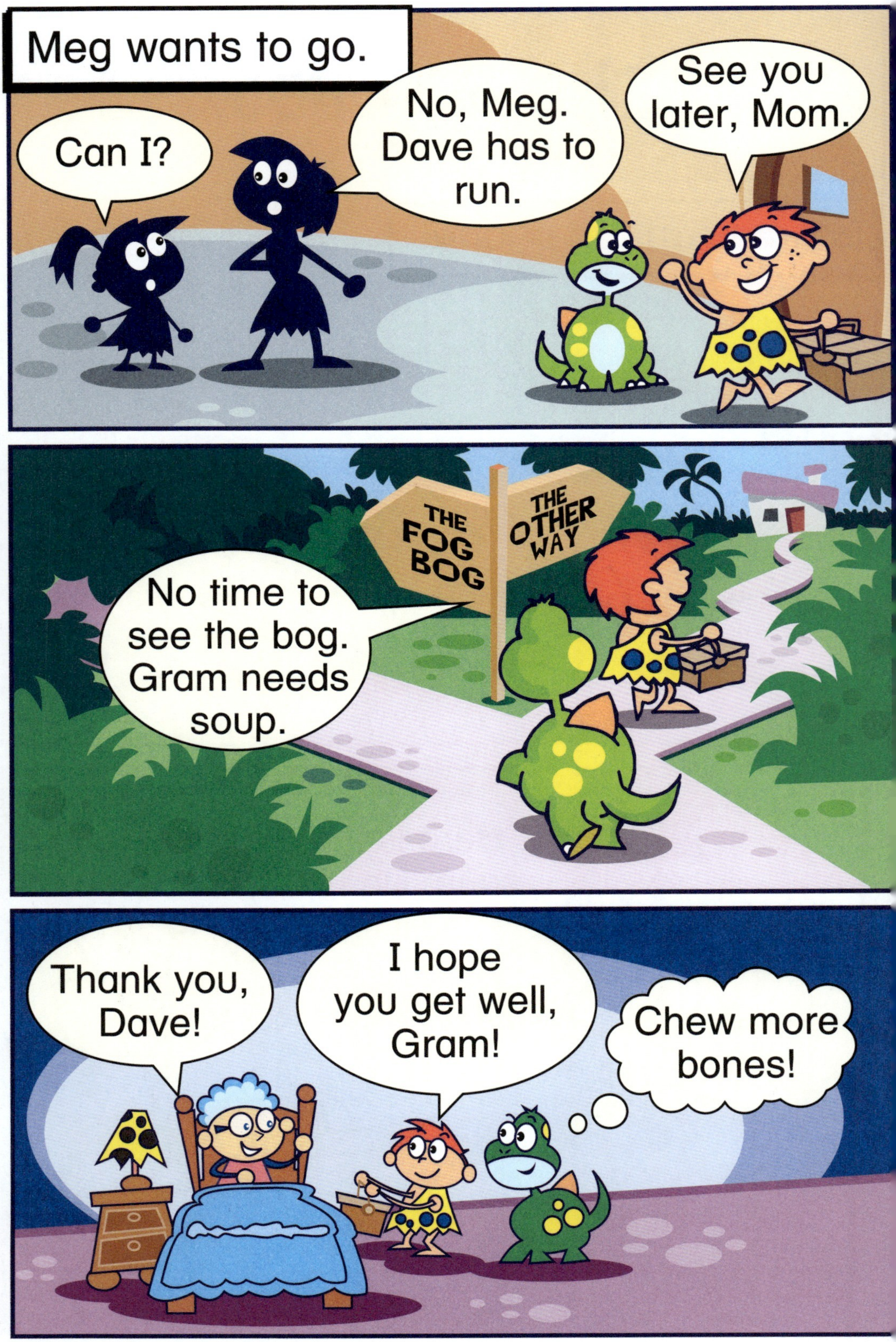
Meg wants to go.
Can I?
No, Meg. Dave has to run.
See you later, Mom.
THE FOG BOG
THE OTHER WAY
No time to see the bog. Gram needs soup.
Thank you, Dave!
I hope you get well, Gram!
Chew more bones!

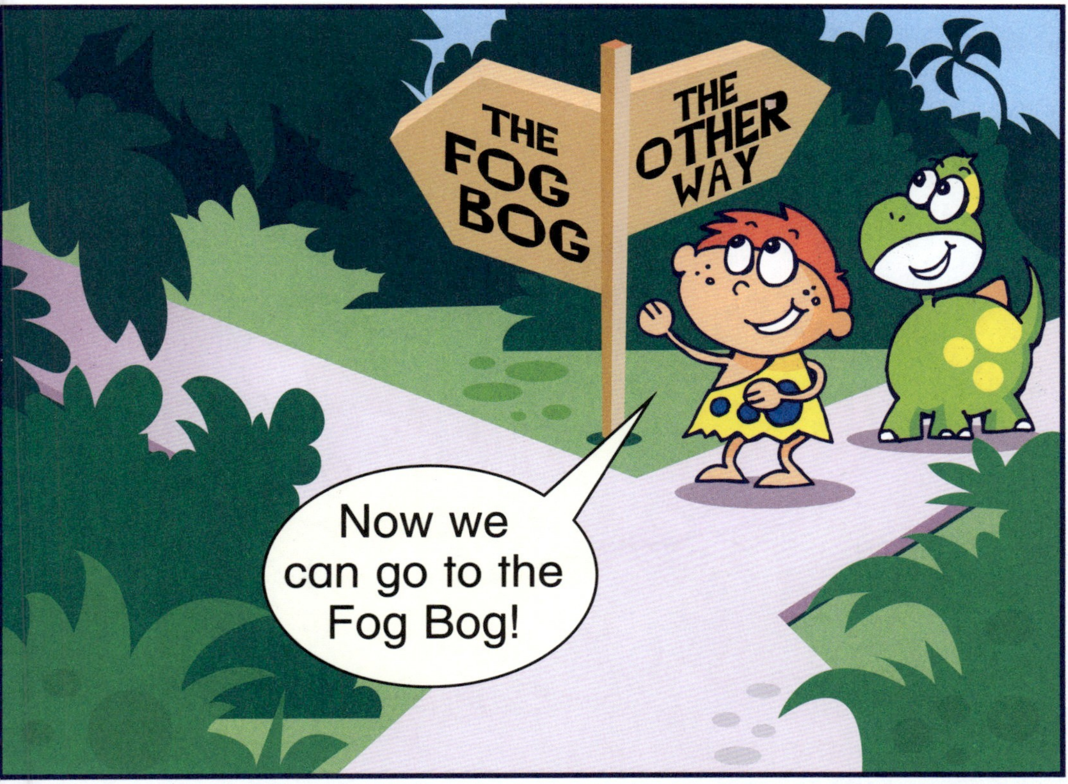
THE FOG BOG
THE OTHER WAY
Now we can go to the Fog Bog!

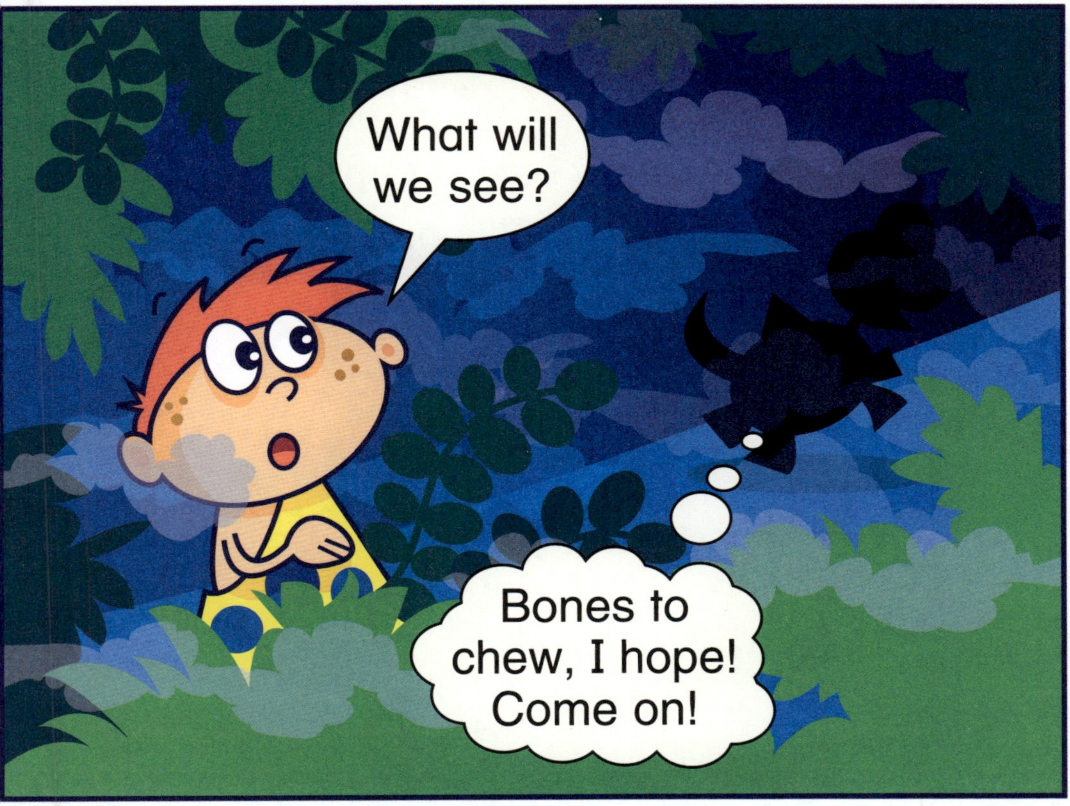
What will we see?
Bones to chew, I hope! Come on!

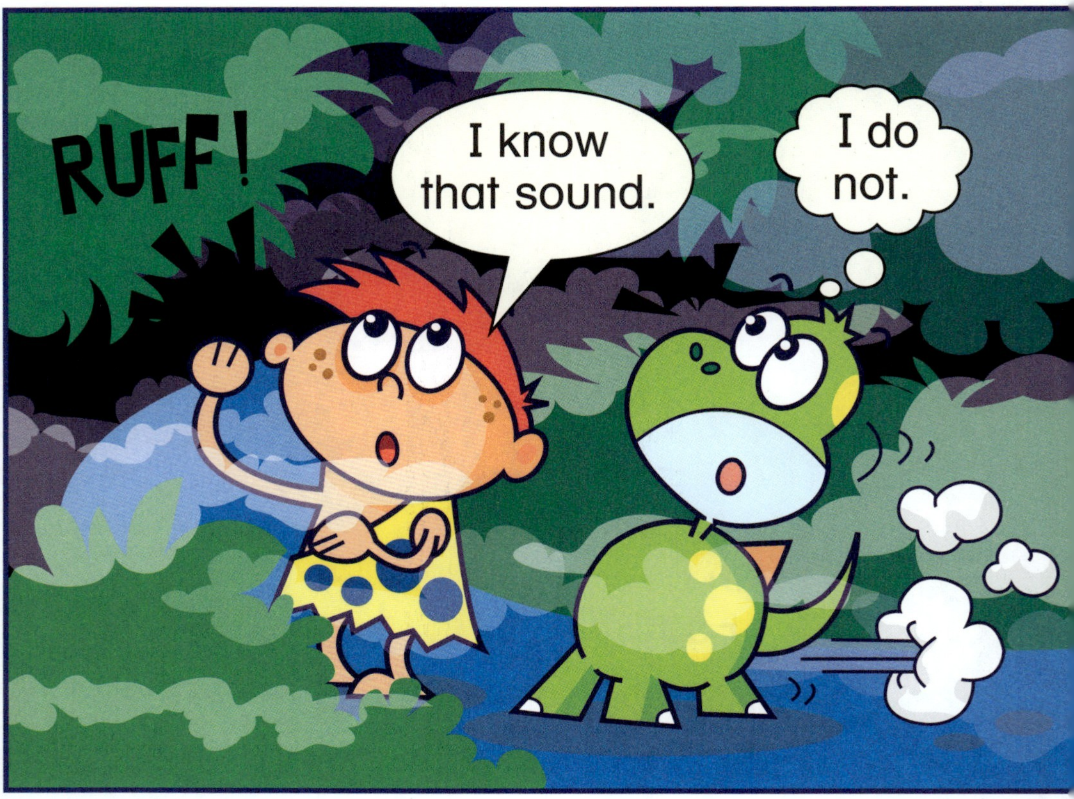
RUFF!
I know that sound.
I do not.

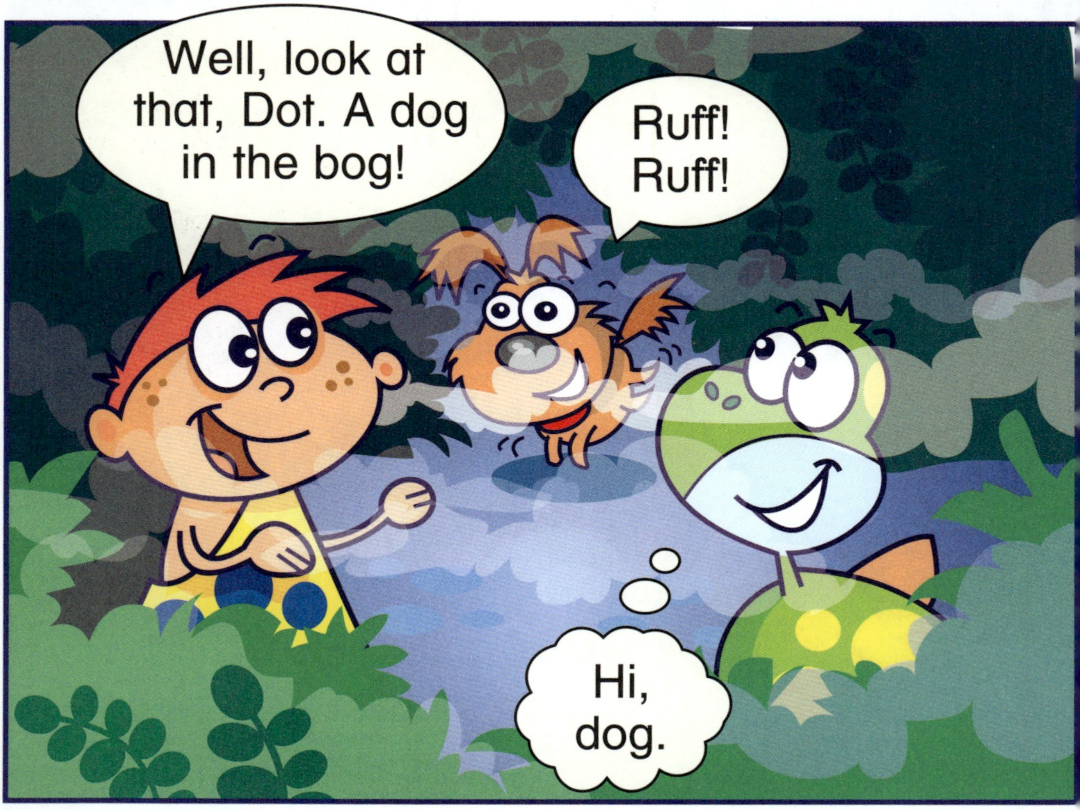
Well, look at that, Dot. A dog in the bog!
Ruff! Ruff!
Hi, dog.

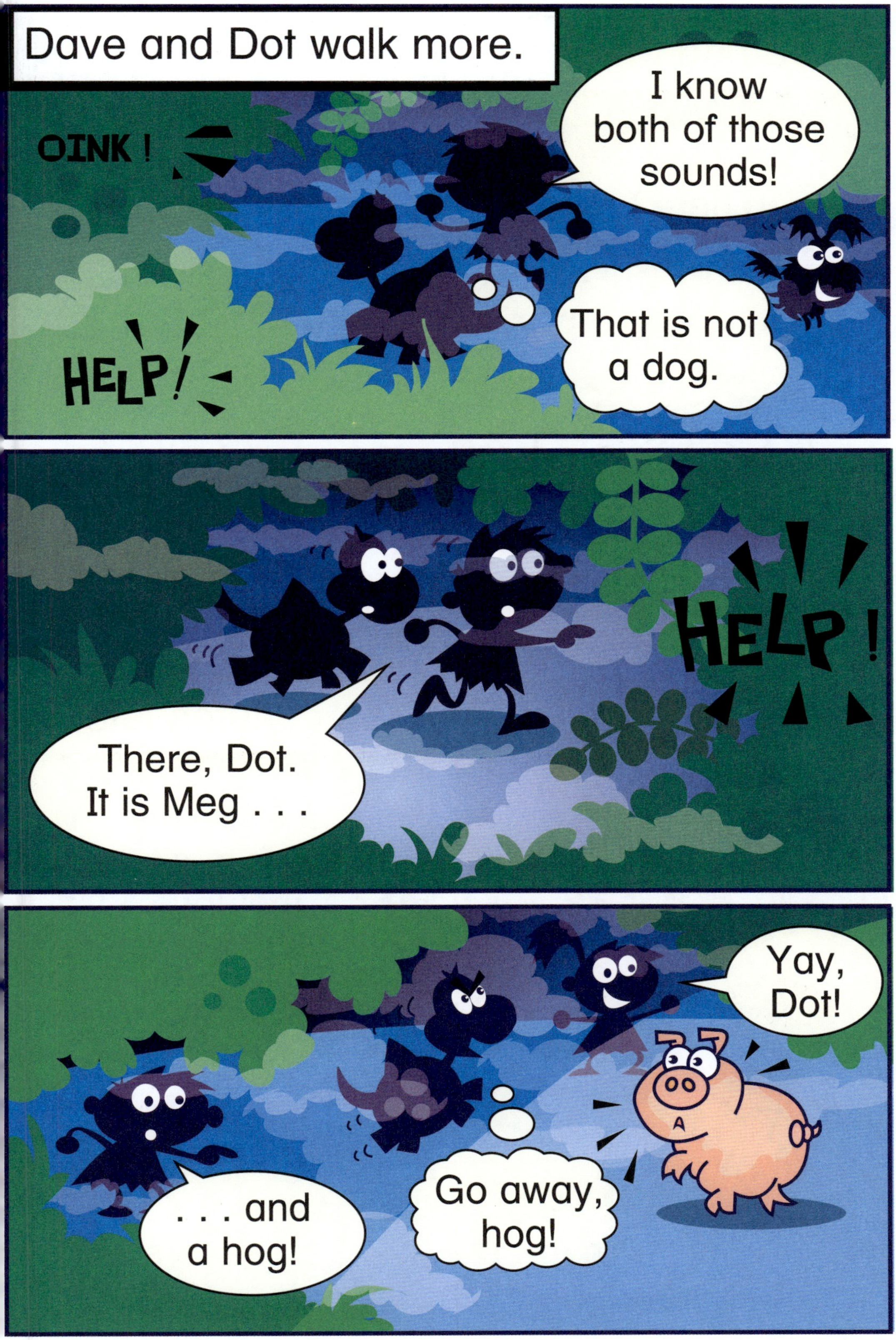
Dave and Dot walk more.
OINK!
HELP!
I know both of those sounds!
That is not a dog.
HELP!
There, Dot. It is Meg . . .
Yay, Dot!
. . . and a hog!
Go away, hog!

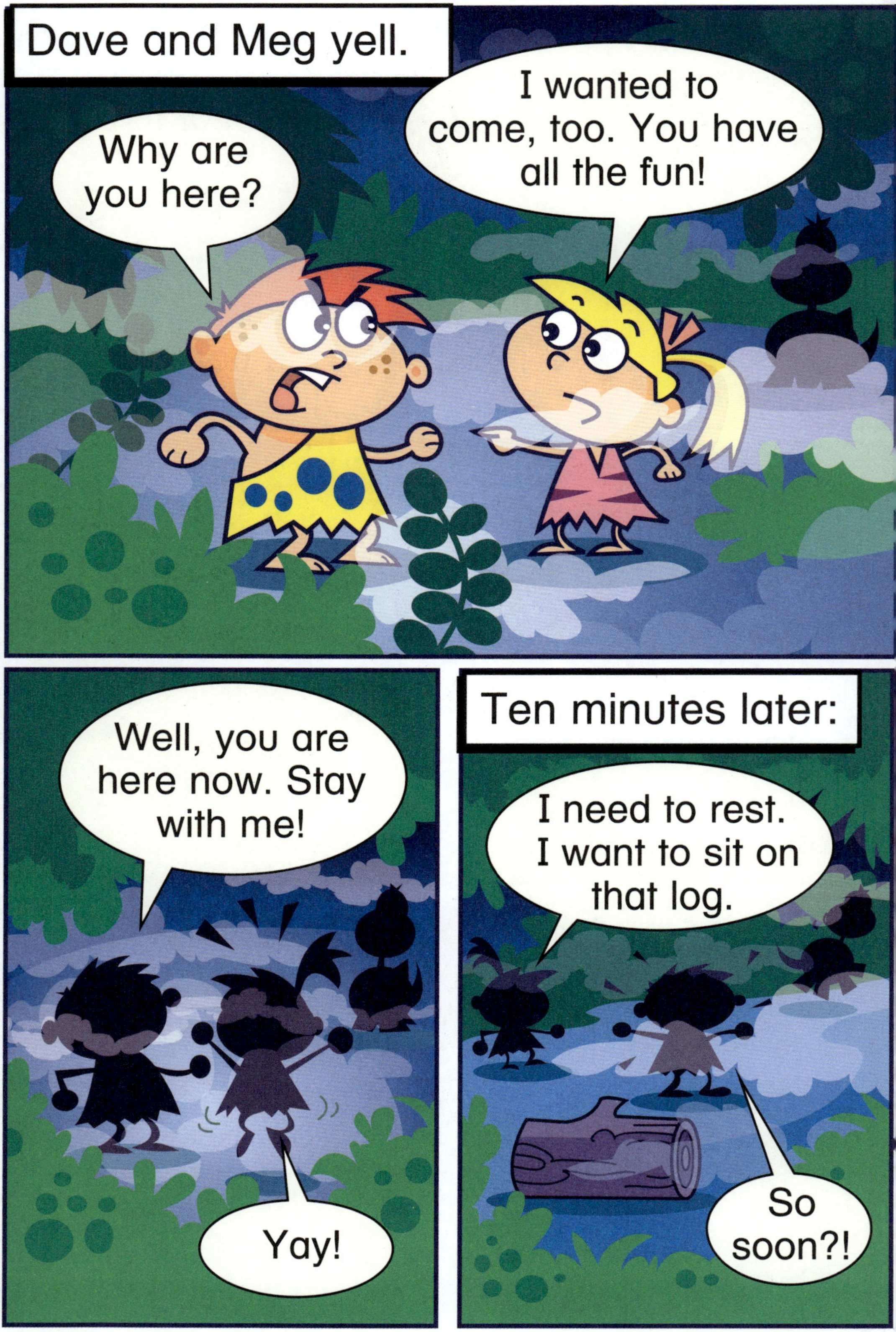
Dave and Meg yell.
Why are you here?
I wanted to come, too. You have all the fun!
Well, you are here now. Stay with me!
Yay!
Ten minutes later:
I need to rest. I want to sit on that log.
So soon?!